DIGITAL DIGIMON MONSTERS™

KARI'S TOUR OF THE Digital World

by Michael Teitelbaum

SCHOLASTIC INC.

New York   Toronto   London   Auckland   Sydney
Mexico City   New Delhi   Hong Kong   Buenos Aires

ISBN 0-439-34112-4

Cover and interior design by Peter Koblish

12 11 10 9 8 7 6 5 4 3   1 2 3 4 5 6/0

Printed in the U.S.A.
First Scholastic printing, October 2001

MEET KARI

Hi! I'm Kari. This is my Digimon pal, Gatomon. I'll tell you more about him in a minute.

THIS IS TAI

This is my brother, Tai, and his Digimon friend, Koromon. I always thought Tai was pretty cool, but I didn't know how cool he really was!

THE ORIGINAL DIGIDESTINED

Tai and his six friends were the original Digidestined. Here are his friends: Sora, Izzy, Mimi, Joe, T.K., and Matt. They were helping to save the Digital World from the forces of evil. They knew there was an eighth Digidestined, but they didn't know who it was.

IT'S KARI!

Then they found out that the eighth Digidestined was me, Kari! Soon I was traveling to the Digital World with them and helping to fight the forces of evil.

GATOMON DIGIVOLVES

Boy, was I surprised when I found out that I was the eighth Digidestined. And then I met Gatomon! Gatomon's In-Training and Rookie stages are Nyaromon and Salamon. Gatomon Digivolves to the Ultimate level Angewoman, and even Armor Digivolves into Nefertimon. But more about that later!

9

SUSPICIONS

My adventure started when Tai and his friends returned from the Digital World. He suspected that I might be the eighth Digidestined.

HOW I FOUND OUT I WAS THE EIGHTH DIGIDESTINED

Gatomon had been under an evil spell cast by Myotismon. When Gatomon's memory returned, she realized that she had been waiting for me all her life. She was destined to be my Digimon companion, and I was Digidestined to be the eighth child, fighting to save the Digital World from evil.

MY DIGIVICE

This is my digivice. It helps me travel back and forth between the real world and the Digital World. But before I finally got to keep it, it was passed around a lot. My cat Miko took it, then a crow had it. The Digimon Wizardmon had it next. He gave it to Gatomon, who was tricked by the evil Myotismon. Pretty weird, huh? But eventually I got it back.

THE DARK MASTERS

I joined the other seven Digidestined kids in the Digital World. My Digipals and I had to battle these four really creepy guys called the Dark Masters. They were four evil Digimon named Piedmon, Machinedramon, MetalSeadramon, and Puppetmon.

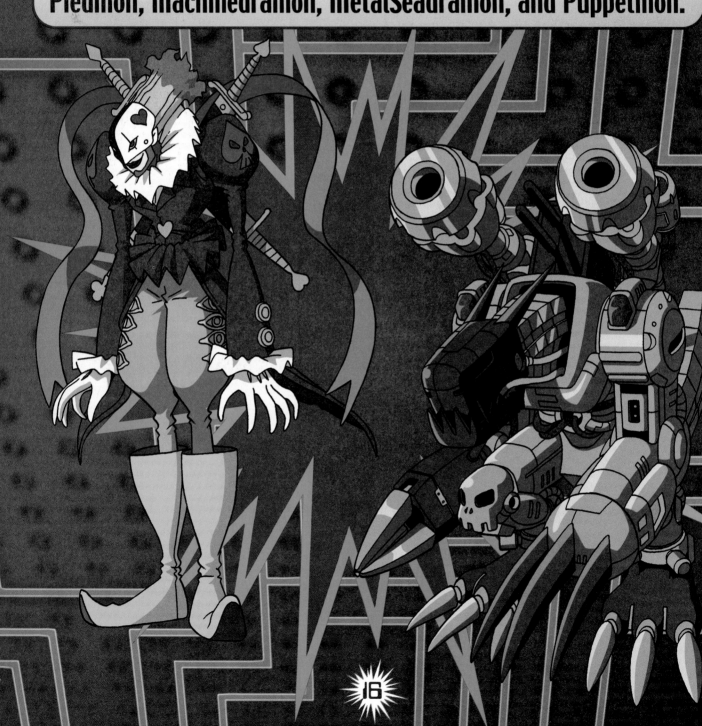

APOCALYMON

Then this really powerful, evil Digimon, Apocalymon, tried to destroy the entire Digital World—with us in it! We looked to the power within ourselves and teamed up to defeat him and save the Digital World.

SAD GOODBYES . . . FOR NOW

We had to say goodbye to our Digimon friends. That was so sad I thought I would cry. I knew I would really miss Gatomon. But somehow, T.K. and I knew that one day we would be reunited with our Digimon pals. And you know what? We were right!

FOUR YEARS LATER

For four years we had no contact with the Digital World. By that time, lots of stuff had happened to my friends. My brother, Tai, was in high school. So was Izzy.

Matt

Tai

Mimi

Mimi moved to New York. Matt joined a band and was trying to become a rock star. Sora became a great tennis player. Joe was studying to become a doctor. And I was four years older, too!

Sora

Izzy

Joe

THE NEW DIGIDESTINED

T.K. and I met three new kids at school—Davis, Yolei, and Cody Hida. Although none of us knew it at the time, they were also Digidestined! I think Davis has a crush on me. He seems jealous that T.K. and I are such good friends.

RETURN TO THE DIGITAL WORLD

Davis got a digivice. It came right through a monitor in the computer lab at school. His digivice looked different from ours. Davis's new digivice opened up the gate to the Digital World. T.K., Davis, and I were transported there.

DIGI-REUNION

In the Digital World we ran into Tai and our Digimon. T.K. was reunited with Patamon. And I got a big hug from my beloved Gatomon! I introduced Davis to my big brother. Davis was kind of freaked out at first by being in the Digital World, but after a while he thought it was cool.

THE EVIL DIGIMON EMPEROR

Gatomon told us all about a really mean kid who called himself the Digimon Emperor. The thing is, he's not a Digimon, he's just a really mean human. This Digimon Emperor captured Digimon. Then he turned them into his evil slaves. Even Gatomon was almost caught!

THE DARK RINGS

The Digimon Emperor used Dark Rings to control the Digimon. This made me really mad! I'd like to slap a ring on him! My friends and I knew that we had to stop this Digimon Emperor.

THE DIGI-EGG OF COURAGE

Deep in a cave, we found the Digi-Egg of Courage. We all tried to lift it, but only Davis was strong enough. That's when Davis met his Digimon companion, Veemon. The Digimon Emperor sent Monochromon to attack us. Using the Digi-Egg of Courage, Veemon Armor Digivolved into Flamedramon. That was the first time I ever saw a Digimon Armor Digivolve. It was pretty amazing. When Flamedramon destroyed the Dark Ring around Monochromon, Monochromon became really nice!

BACK THROUGH THE GATE

After our first adventure as a new team, T.K., Davis, and I traveled back though the Digital Gate and returned to the real world. Cody and Yolei were waiting in the computer lab with Izzy.

THE DIGI-TEAM COMPLETED!

Two more of the new-style digivices popped through the computer monitor, right into the hands of Yolei and Cody. The gate opened, and T.K. and I, along with Davis, Cody, and Yolei, returned to the Digital World. We're the five Digidestined and we're a real team!

EVERYONE'S GOT A DIGIMON

Yolei found the Digi-Egg of Love. When she picked it up, she met Hawkmon, who had been waiting for her. Then Cody found the Digi-Egg of Knowledge. He met Dillomon, who had been waiting for him. Now we all have a Digimon partner, and our team is really complete!

MORE DIGI-EGGS

I found the Digi-Egg of Light deep in a cave. T.K found the Digi-Egg of Hope.

TIME TO ARMOR DIGIVOLVE

Using the Digi-Egg of Light, Gatomon Armor Digivolved into Nefertimon, a powerful, flying Digimon. T.K.'s Digi-Egg of Hope helped Patamon Armor Digivolve into Pegasusmon. I went for a ride in the sky on Nefertimon. Now I don't have to walk all over the Digital World!

DESTROY THE SPIRES!

I learned that the Control Spires all over the Digital World were the key to the Digimon Emperor's power. The Control Spires control the Dark Rings, and the Dark Rings control the Digimon! We have to destroy all the Control Spires to stop the Digimon Emperor! Flying on Nefertimon, I destroyed one. That helped all the Digimon in the area to Digivolve again.

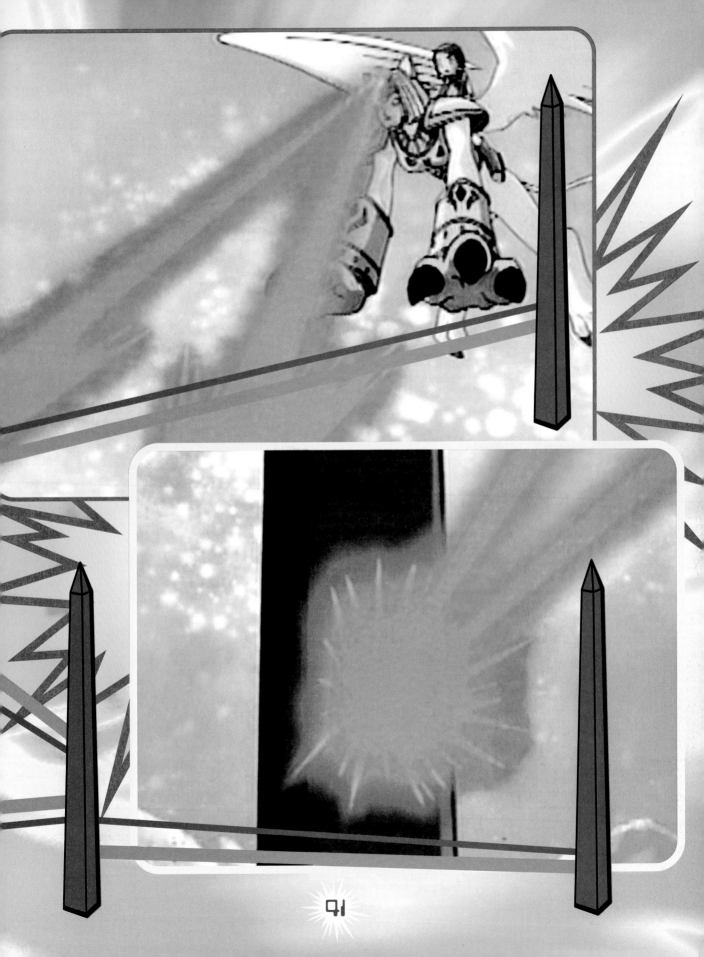

THE EMPEROR'S EVIL DIGIMON

During my time in the Digital World, the Digital Emperor sent lots of evil Digimon to attack us. After Monochromon, he sent Tyrannomon, Snimon, Mojyamon, Redveggiemon, Ebidramon, and lots of others.

THE DIGIMON EMPEROR REVEALED!

At last we learned who the Digimon Emperor really was. And boy were we surprised! The Digimon Emperor is a kid named Ken Ichijoji, a world-famous computer genius and champion soccer player. Here's how we found out. In the real world, Davis played against Ken in a soccer game. He accidentally kicked Ken in the shin, and cut his leg. Later, while battling the Digimon Emperor in the Digital World, Davis saw the very same cut on the leg of the Digimon Emperor!

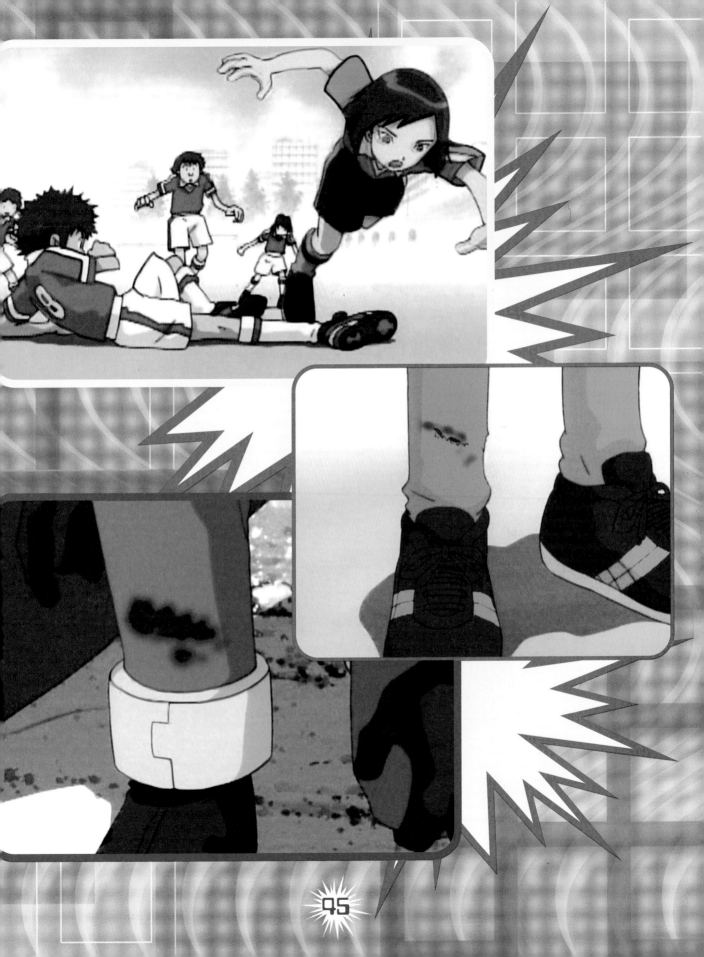

VICTORY!

It turns out that Ken thought that the Digital World was nothing but his own personal video game. A long time ago, Ken's brother died. He was so sad that he would hide in the Digital World, and pretend it was a game. When Ken realized that he was truly hurting Digimon, he gave up being the Digimon Emperor.

FRIENDS!

We finally forgave Ken, and asked him to be our friend. He now helps us in our battle against evil. I like going to school, but I love my trips to the Digital World, too. I'm a lucky girl. You might say I have the best of both worlds!